"Laws are like cobwebs, for if any trifling or
powerless thing falls into them, they hold it fast; but
if a thing of any size falls into them it breaks the
mesh and escapes."

— ANACHARSIS (c. 600 B.C.)

"Law and order are always and everywhere the law
and order which protect the established hierarchy."

— HERBERT MARCUSE (1898-1979)

"If you have the right eye for these things, you can
see that accused men are often attractive."

— FRANZ KAFKA (1883-1924)

writer ALAN MOORE • *artist* EDDIE CAMPBELL

art assistance PETE MULLINS • *logo* TODD KLEIN
chapter heading calligraphy DES RODE • *design and production* DOUGLAS BANTZ
editors PHILIP AMARA AND CHRIS COUCH • *art director* AMIE BROCKWAY

publisher DENIS KITCHEN • *vp, production* JIM KITCHEN
vp, business affairs and operations SCOTT HYMAN • *vp, chief financial officer* DEAN ZIROLLI
sales and marketing director JAMIE RIEHLE • *sales manager* GAIL "ZIGGY" ZYGMONT
customer service manager KAREN LOWMAN • *managing editor* JOHN WILLS • *warehouse managers* VIC LISEWSKI
Printed in Canada

Chapter Twelve

The Apprehensions of Mr Lees

No. We are merely troubled by a moment's melancholia. Besides, Sir William is himself unwell and given over to strange moods of late.

We fear that any further strain or upset on the Doctor may invite disaster. Do you know Sir William, Mr. Lees?

I am similarly familiar with your work, sir, profiting from delusions born of bereavement. Consequently, I have relished this meeting not at all. Good day.

I know the Doctor only a little, Your Majesty. I am sorry to hear that he is indisposed.

Is there someone else I should summon?

If we require it, we shall send for Dr. Treves, but for the moment we would soonest be alone.

Of course. Until next time, Your majesty.

Excuse me, but I wondered if you might assist me? I am informed by Her Majesty that my dear friend, Sir William Gull, is ailing.

Indeed? I am similarly familiar with YOUR work, sir, profiting from delusions born of bereavement.

Consequently, I have relished this meeting not at all. Good day.

'E was goin' on about doctors an' brooks full of blood... Put the wind up me somethin' rotten.

Uhhhrr

Mr. Lees? Mr. Lees, are you alright.?

Whuhh... Wh-where AM I?

You're in a police station, sir, and I'm Inspector Abberline. We were just talking when you 'ad a fit.

Y-yes. Yes. I remember now...

The visions. The terrible visions.

D-Did I say anything? While I was in the trance, did I speak to you?

Uh, well, you were talking about a doctor, sir. And a brook.

Oh God: the brook! I remember...

In my vision it was bubbling up from the ground, somewhere in West London. It was blood, Inspector, human blood.

A- and the KILLER. I could SEE him. H-he was a DOCTOR.

He killed those women with a doctor's knife

These fearful waking dreams. If only I were rid of them!

But how, knowing the fiend may strike again while I am helpless to prevent it?

Uh, look, I suppose we could investigate this, if only to put your mind at rest. No harm done if you're wrong, eh?

Godley, can you have somebody fetch us a carriage.

It's for me and Mr. Lees. We're going up west.

We're comin' up to Grosvenor Square. Bit posh for a killer, surely?

I disagree! How APT that one who preys upon the working classes should be WEALTHY!

Hmmph. I see, sir. Bit of a FABIAN, are we?

I am indeed of that society, and I believe that... WAIT! I'm GETTING something. Make him stop the cab.

OY! MATE! This'll do 'ere. You can pull over.

S- so strong. The images are so strong. Blood. Knives. The screaming of women. Make them STOP.

Well, we'll do our best, eh? Driver, you wait 'ere. I'm sure we shan't be long.

Right. D'you feel well enough to go through with this, Mr. Lees, or should we...?

No, No. I must be strong, even in the jaws of evil.

I-I think we should go THIS way. I can hear the awful gurgling of the blood-red brook somewhere ahead...

Look, mr. Lees, I don't know about this. If you're larkin' about...

Inspector, I promise you I am quite serious. Knock on the door and we'll SEE.

hahhh Alright, then, sir. If you insist.

yes?

um, I'm Inspector Abberline of Scotland Yard. This gentleman is a, uh, psychic investigator.

Look, I wonder if we could see the MASTER of the 'ouse.

Charlotte? Who are you talking to?

Two callers, ma'am. one's a policeman and one of 'ems Psychic. They want the master.

My husband is not well at present, and cannot receive any guests. If you'll tell me your business, Inspector..

Abberline, ma'am. Scotland Yard.

I- it's about an enquiry which we're pursuing. If we could just have a few moments, I'm sure that we won't need to bother you further.

This is a great inconvenience, Inspector.

oh, very well. Come inside if you must, but I'll warn you I cannot spare long.

No, ma'am. Thank you, ma'am.

S- Sir William Gull?

Of COURSE Sir William Gull! Who did you THINK you were harassing? And over such SORDID little crimes! It's utterly OUTRAGEOUS!

Lady Gull, please, we simply wanted to...

To know where my husband was on the night of the MURDERS? To implicate the finest surgeon in England with BUTCHERY?

Your ladyship, please...

What if he WASN'T home? My husband is a DOCTOR, Inspector. He's OFTEN called out in the evenings! Really, this is TOO bad.

A-as for his BEHAVIOUR...

Inspector, my husband isn't well. You must understand, he had a terrible heart-seizure almost a year ago. It affected him DREADFULLY.

Please, your ladyship, there's no need...

I mean, of COURSE I've been worried about him. Sometimes he seems so REMOTE. 1- It's as if I hardly know him.

Poor Susan, do not fret. All shall be well. My GREETINGS gentlemen.

I am Sir William Withey Gull.

How may I HELP you?

look, I'm uh... I'm sorry about this, Sir William. It's just that, well, we had information about... w-well, about the MURDERS in WHITECHAPEL.

I mean, it's SILLY, I know, but... well, y'know, we 'ave to check these things out, and... Y'see, what it is, somebody thought you were the CULPRIT.

I am.

That is, I think I MUST be. Up until the one in Miller's Court, events were all so VIVID, but since then...

Since then, things seem so VAGUE and GHOSTLY.

I DO distinctly recollect awakening to find my shirt cuffs stiff with blood. And there were the most strange and wonderful of dreams...

oh, William. oh, dear GOD.

I KNEW, William. Somehow, I KNEW.

yes, yes, I suppose you did. Dear Susan, you have been the best of wives to me.

Would that I might have spared you this. Would that I might have told you something of my task. I could not. You would not have understood.

Forgive me.

Er...

Oh christ.

What the fuck do I do now?

I mean é's the fuckin Royal DOCTOR! He's right next to HER MAJESTY! He's... he's the one who...

oh fuck

W-we have to tell somebody. Scotland Yard. We have to go to Scotland Yard

Our Cab. It's waiting for us.

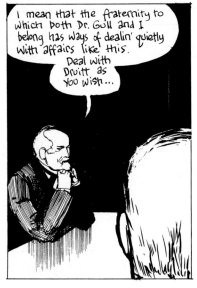

yes?

we have come for Brother Gull.

H-Her ladyship said that her and the master weren't to be disturbed.

It's alright, Charlotte.

I've been expecting them. Allow me, gentlemen, a moment to put on my coat. I shall be with you presently.

From Hell - Chapter 12 page 18

From Hell - chapter 12 - page 19

Who seeks admittance, Master Tyler?

They have brought the Knight of the East, most worshipful master.

Enter, Knight of the East.

Knight of the East, do you solemnly swear to always hele, conceal and never reveal the rites of the Free and Accepted Masons?

I do.

Very well. We are gathered here beneath the God of Love and before the sight of the Great Architect to judge this case.

Let the hearing commence.

Knight of the East, you stand accused of mayhems that have placed our brotherhood in jeopardy, before your peers, masons and doctors both.

I have no peers here present.

What?

I fancy that you understand me, sir.

There is no man amongst you fit to judge the mighty Act that I have wrought.

Your rituals are empty oaths you neither understand nor live by. You cite the Great Architect yet would befoul yourselves should he ADDRESS you.

But he does NOT address you. Not Westcott there, nor Woodford by his side, for all their mummery. Not Dr. Howard, ever in his cups.

And yet he speaks to ME. He is the balance where my deeds are weighed and judged.

Not you.

Sir William, this is insufferable.

You do not seem to understand the seriousness of this charge. I fear that you are suffering from DELUSIONS.

Indeed?

Fear, rather, that I'm NOT.

We have to deal with this. Sir William's clearly quite insane and further hearings would be pointless.

What are we to DO with him?

He can't remain at large. That's plain as day, yet neither can we lock him up.

You're not suggesting that he should be executed?

Of course not! Why, this is Sir William Gull we're speaking of!

What if he were to die of natural causes?

I doubt he'll do it soon. Despite his mental frailty he's stronger than an ox.

Of course, he could APPEAR to have passed on.

What do you mean?

I mean we could perhaps fake his demise, then spirit him away somewhere.

We'd need a death certificate signed by two doctors.

We could get away with ONE. Isn't Gull's son-in-law a doctor? Young Dyke-Acland?

Gentlemen please. This is not an occasion for levity. Our plan may take months to accomplish. Perhaps even longer. We need stop-gap remedies also.

As I said, we'll place Gull under watch. Beyond that, what do you suggest?

That rumours should come into circulation to confuse the scent.

Say, for example, that the murderer were a deranged young man who took his own life after concluding the crime

...By drowning

...In the Thames.

THORNEYCROFT TORPEDO WORKS

"It is an old maxim of mine that when you have excluded the impossible, whatever remains, however improbable, must be the truth."

— SIR ARTHUR CONAN DOYLE (1859-1930)

"Whatever is almost true is quite false, and among the most dangerous of errors, because being so near truth, it is the more likely to lead astray."

— HENRY WARD BEECHER (1813-1887)

Chapter Thirteen

A Return to Cleveland Street

Aft'noon, sir. 'ow can I 'elp yer?

I don't know, yet. For a start I'll 'ave a quarter o' them acid drops up there.

Worked 'ere long, 'ave yer?

Long enough. Mrs. Morgan, who owns the shop, she's my mum. Why d'ye wanna know, anyway?

Because I'm a Police officer, son, and knowin's my job.

The house across the street, number thirteen. They come in 'ere much?

Oh, THEM. well, I daresay we all know what goes on there, don't we? Yeah, we 'ave the mollies in 'ere now and again.

From Hell - Chapter 13 - page 3

Sweet cachous, mostly, for their breath.

Some of the Gents we've 'ad in 'ere, you'd be surprised.

Really? OW surprised?

VERY surprised, I should think. I'm not talking about your ordinary brown-hatter, mind.

Hmm. Prince Albert Victor. We're aware of 'im. You're sayin' 'e comes in 'ere then?

Oh, Don't 'e just! Been comin' in 'ere for years 'e 'as.

Is that right?

Right as I'm standin' 'ere. I'll tell yer what, though, it's not all bum-boys for 'is 'ighness. Likes girls as well, 'e does.

You're sure it's not chaps dressed up? They've got them over there as well y'know.

No, this was a girl who used to work here.

Annie Crook 'er name was. Ever such a scandal. They reckon she 'ad 'is baby, but it were kept quiet. There. Just over. Is that alright?

That's fine. 'Ad 'is baby? A sweet shop girl? You're 'avin' me on.

God's truth. There was another girl worked 'ere; looked after it for 'em.

Little Irish girl. I forget what 'er name was. Mary something. Or Marie. Pretty little thing. That'll be tuppence three farthing.

Hm. Well it's a good yarn. I'll grant yer that. P'raps I'll pop in and 'ave a chat wi' you again sometime.

Goodbye for now.

From Hell-Chapter 13-page 4

Blimey, you're back quick. Forget something did yer?

The little Irish girl who looked after this baby; 'Er second name weren't Kelly, was it?

From Hell·chapter 13·page 6

...in which case we'll need more officers in the street before...

Abberline, what in God's name d'ye think yer playin' at, man, bargin' into my office!

It's about the Whitechapel Case.

Sir.

I see.

Gentlemen, if you could leave the Inspector and myself alone for a minute.

Right. They're gone. Now, what the Hell is this all about?

A Royal baby. And its nursemaid.

Girl named Kelly.

oh dear.

Oh dear? Oh DEAR?. You told me Gull was MAD. That 'e'd just murdered these women on a WHIM. You never told me 'e 'ad REASONS.

I mean, what was it? Threaten to talk, did she? You KNEW. From the first murder you KNEW, and you let us carry on INVESTIGATIN'.

I suppose that's why I got this CLEVELAND STREET job! You thought if I'd been cunt enough to keep me trap shut ONCE, I'd do it AGAIN.'

Abberline...

'e'll just get off, won't 'e, Gull? You won't lay a finger on 'im, you'll...

Abberline, listen to me.

Gull WAS insane. We're considering locking him away. Nobody expected him to do what he did. All the same, we have to live with it.

We live with it, and we say nothing. Not me, not you, not your silly little clairvoyant friend, Mr. Lees

If asked, we make something up.

A barrister called Druitt was pulled out of the Thames around New Year. Perhaps HE was yer Ripper now?

Tell 'em any name ye want, save Gull's.

Now, you've been frank with me, so I'll be frank with you. You'll keep your mouths shut, you and Lees, and draw a generous PENSION for it.

Breathe a word to anyone and ye'll not reach retirement. D'ye follow me, now?

Sir, I wish to give notice of my retirement from the force at the earliest convenient date.

Whatever you wish. It changes nothing that I've said.

Perhaps you'd like to take the rest of the day off and think things over, now —

Goodbye, Mr. Anderson.

Goodbye now, Inspector.

W. C.

OFFICERS ONLY

hhuch
Ghuhuh

APPENDIX TO VOLUME NINE:

CHAPTER TWELVE

PAGES 1-15

Since most of the events in this chapter issue from a single source, this being Stephen Knight's *JTR: The Final Solution*, there seems little need to give separate page references. However, some of the strands of the narrative, as suggested by Knight and as interpreted here, are in need of explanation.

It seems that the story of Jack the Ripper's unveiling at the hands of the alleged psychic Robert Lees is of somewhat uncertain origin. The only piece of concrete evidence linking Lees to the case at all is one of the anonymous letters from presumably wanna-be Rippers that Scotland Yard received on the 25th of July, 1889. It read, in part, as follows:

> Dear Boss
> You have not caught me yet you see, with all your cunning, with all your "Lees" and blue bottles.

This seems to support the idea that by 1889, Lees's name had indeed become somehow associated with the case, at least by rumor. The next shred of confirming evidence turns up in the Chicago *Sunday Times-Herald* on the 28th of April, 1895. This recounted a story allegedly told by a London physician, Dr. Benjamin Howard, in which it was stated that the psychic Robert Lees had led a police inspector to the home of a prominent physician in the West End of London. The piece never mentions William Gull by name, but lines such as "He had been ever since he was a student at Guy's Hospital, an ardent and enthusiastic vivisectionist" are certainly suggestive of the good doctor, jibing as they do with the reported facts

of his life and opinions.

According to the account in the *Sunday Times-Herald*, the psychic and the policemen were initially met by the doctor's wife, who, although angrily issuing denials at first, soon admitted that there had been moments lately when she worried about her husband's behavior, and that he had indeed been absent on the nights of the murders. It is at this point that the doctor himself entered, and confessed that upon several occasions he had woken to find his shirt stained with blood.

Dr. Howard's purported account goes on to describe that secret trial that we see in the second half of this chapter. I say "purported" because there seems to be some dispute over whether Dr. Benjamin Howard had any connection with the article at all. Dr. Howard himself wrote a furious denial when the story was reprinted in England's Sunday tabloid, *The People*. Ripperologist Melvin Harris has made a case for the possibility that the whole story was invented by the Chicago Whitechapel Club who used to hold meetings in a back room at the offices of the *Sunday Times-Herald*.

This would seem to assume that someone associated with the Chicago Whitechapel Club had somehow stumbled across the obscure historical snippet that Robert Lees had been thought to have some connection with the Whitechapel case. From this fragment, they had cleverly concocted a story that dragged in a real physician, Dr. Howard, who it seems was indeed in America at the time, being American by birth. It's possible, of course, that the name "Dr. Howard" was invented by the hoaxers and had only coincidental connection to a real London physician who fitted its particulars in almost every detail, but this does seem to be stretching coincidence a bit far.

The hoaxers had also, presumably accidentally, included a description of the alleged murderer that fitted exactly with William Gull. Since as far as I know Sir William's name had been nowhere associated with the crime by 1895, we must again presume this to be a coincidence if we are to conclude that the *Times-Herald* piece was indeed a hoax.

My own feeling is that while the story has many hoax-like qualities, the number of supporting stories that have accumulated around it from varying sources place it in a somewhat different category. If it *is* a hoax, it's a rather peculiar one that seems to have a diverse range of contributors adding to it across the last hundred years.

According to Cynthia Legh, a person who'd known Lees since 1912 and who was interviewed in *Light, The Journal of the College of Psychic Studies* in the autumn of 1970, she had heard him tell basically the same story with minor variations on dozens of occasions. Ms. Legh, of course, could have invented this after reading the *Times-Herald* story. Similarly, Lees himself could have simply read the *Times-Herald* story and decided to play along with it for reasons of personal vanity. The hoax theory is of course still perfectly plausible, but seems to become more tenuous with each new coincidence or poorly-motivated sub-hoax that it had to absorb.

1970 also saw the publication of an issue of *The Criminologist* in which a Dr. Thomas Stowell claimed to have been told a story by a Mrs. Caroline Acland:

She was the wife of Theodore Dyke Acland, M.D., F.R.C.P., one time my beloved Chief. I knew them both intimately and often enjoyed the hospitality of their home in Bryanston Square over many years.

It will be remembered that Caroline Acland was the daughter of Sir William Gull. Stowell went on to recount the following:

Mrs. Acland's story was that at the time of the Ripper murders, her Mother, Lady Gull, was greatly annoyed one night by an unappointed visit from a police officer, accompanied by a man who called himself a medium and she was irritated by their impudence in asking her a number of questions which seemed to her impertinent . . . Later Sir William himself came down and, in answer to the questions, said Gull occasionally suffered from "lapses of memory since he had a slight stroke in 1887"; he said that he had once discovered blood on his shirt.

Now, either this dovetails with Lees's story due to another credibility-stretching coincidence, or we must assume that either Caroline Acland, for some reason, wished to contribute to the hoax by implicating her own father. Or, failing that, that Stowell himself wished to contribute to the hoax, and in doing so implicated the respected father of his close and intimate friends, the Aclands.

Sadly, we cannot question Dr. Stowell himself on these issues as the high-ranking Freemason apparently died shortly after this revealing article was published. Funnily enough, he died on November 9th, the anniversary of Mary Kelly's murder.

Later, of course, Walter Sickert's alleged illegitimate son, Joseph "Hobo" Sickert, would add his own contributions to this extraordinary story, but these will be dealt with in the proposed second appendix to *From Hell*, "The Dance of the Gull-Catchers."

What we are left with, for the moment, is a fascinating story that seems to emanate from numerous (albeit suspect) sources, and which has very little to actually disprove it. The scenes depicted in the first fifteen pages here are my own interpretation of those rumored events, tailored to fit in with my own feelings concerning Lees's possibly base motivations. If Lees was indeed Victoria's psychic, then he should have been able to recognize the Queen's famous physician when he allegedly glimpsed the Ripper while riding a London bus. My own interpretation is more in keeping with my perception of Lees as suggested in the prologue to *From Hell*: "I made it all up, and it all came true anyway."

The dialogue here, as well as the reactions of Lees, Abberline, and Abberline's superiors at Scotland Yard, is of course invented.

P A G E S   1 6   -   2 6

The second part of our story also originates with the purported Dr. Howard *Times-Herald* account, in which it states that a secret trial was held before a jury composed of twelve London physicians, during which the accused was found to be insane and removed to an insane asylum in Islington. His death was faked, and a sham burial service carried out. The setting of the trial in this episode is based on the tantalizing piece of information revealed in *London Under London*, by Richard Trench and Ellis Hillman (John Murray, Ltd., 1984), which states that there still exists a Masonic temple directly under Piccadilly Circus, famous for its statue of Eros, with an entrance through the cellars of a nearby Bistro. I decided that this would make a poignant locale for the trial of Gull, although I must admit that the decor is drawn purely from the imagination, since no photographs of this particular meeting place are known to exist.

The various members of the jury were chosen by virtue of their being Doctors, Freemasons, and active in London at that time. Dr. Benjamin Howard seemed an obvious choice given the *Times-Herald* story in which Howard claimed to have been present at the trial. Dr. Robert Anderson was included to preserve the Police connection, while Drs. Woodford and

Westcott, besides being doctors with Freemasonic connections of that period, were included because of their association with the only-recently founded Order of the Golden Dawn and my own fondness for introducing arcane historical celebrities at the drop of a hat.

According to Stephen Knight, the only signature upon Gull's death certificate was that of his son-in-law, Theodore Dyke Acland, which was a highly irregular state of affairs. Also according to Knight, Gull's official funeral at his family home of Thorpe le Soken in 1890 involved a coffin full of stones substituted for the body, with the real Gull spirited away to the Islington asylum under the name of "Thomas Mason, alias number 124." Knight suggests that Gull actually died at the asylum in 1896, whereupon his body would have been secretly buried, reunited with his wife and that coffin full of stones. Knight reports that Gull's grave at Thorpe le Soken is said to be unusually wide, implying the possibility that there may indeed be three coffins buried there, although to be frank, an Exhumation Order is unlikely on such scant evidence.

C H A P T E R   T H I R T E E N

As with the previous chapter, there are only at the most one or two sources for the narrative presented here, which makes the usual precise itemization pointless and unnecessary. Abberline's return to Cleveland Street during the summer months of 1889 is documented in Michael Harrison's book *Clarence* (W.H. Allen, 1972).

Abberline was a part of the team that investigated the notorious male brothel kept at number 19, Cleveland Street by one Charles Hammond. The investigation was politically sensitive by virtue of the fact that a recurring customer at Hammond's brothel was Prince Albert Victor Christian

Edward, the Prince Eddy of our narrative. In police notes
and reports pertaining to the case, all references to the
prince are abbreviated into P. A. V. (Prince Albert Victor).
Lord Arthur Somerset, another politically tricky customer
and prominent aristocrat, was also implicated in the
evidence of the police.

It is known that the police did interview the staff and the
proprietors of Mrs. Morgan's sweetshop, just across the road,
about their observations of the brothel.

Abberline's specific conversation with the young man at the
sweet shop is made up, but, as usual, is hung precariously
upon a fragment of reported fact. In a book published in
Paris, 1910, by the Great Beast, Tomegatherion 666, Aleister
Crowley (not himself a stranger to these pages) and entitled
The World's Tragedy, it is claimed that Crowley was in the
receipt of letters written by Prince Albert Victor to a boy
called Morgan, son of Mrs. Morgan, owner of the sweetshop
on Cleveland Street where Annie Crook once worked.

Given that the affair on Cleveland Street pertaining to the
brothel was the last significant or major case that Abberline
worked on before his some-have-said abrupt retirement from
the police force, it seemed possible that Abberline might
have received the final missing pieces of the Jack the Ripper
jigsaw while making investigations at the sweetshop.

Abberline's subsequent conversation with Robert Anderson
on pages 7–10 is an invention, although loosely based upon
the cover-up conspiracy notion that was first put forward in
Knight's *JTR: The Final Solution*, which implies that Abberline
may have received a special pension in order to buy his
silence. Other authors have disputed this and pointed out
that Abberline probably took an early retirement just to take
advantage of a new police retirement scheme, and that his
pension was not greater than what any senior officer of his
rank might be expected to receive.

The visit made to Mr. Lees's house is likewise invented, but
is once again based on a snippet with its origins in Stephen
Knight's incendiary book. Knight claims that Lees had
family in Bournemouth, the resort to which the Abberlines
eventually retired, with a Bournemouth solicitor named
Nelson Lees who was appointed Abberline's executor.
Extrapolating from this, Knight infers that Lees and
Abberline may have both kept in contact until later life, the
scene here meant to lay the groundwork for that possibility.

The final pages, with the disillusioned Abberline discovering
the Pinkerton card given to him several chapters back by
Buffalo Bill stand-in Mexico Joe, are related to the job that
Abberline took up after his resignation from the police force.
Working for the Pinkerton Agency, Abberline cleaned up
the gambling casinos of Monaco. Strangely, in his later
writings on his own life, Abberline dwells for the most part
on his admittedly impressive Monaco experiences.

The Whitechapel crimes and Jack the Ripper hardly get a
mention.

KNOW MADNESS

From Hell

MAD LOVE

Alan Moore and Eddie Campbell's
Award-Winning Tale of Jack the Ripper